Come Back, Bear

Gerald Locklin

Spout Hill Press

Published January 2013

ISBN: 978-0615736181

Spout Hill Press
Walnut, California
SpoutHillPress.com

To all those whose names I have taken in vain within the following pages, and to Ann and John Brantingham who have given you a chance to read this book and for me to re-read what I wrote about twenty-five years ago, and, finally, to see it in print.

And to my father, who was everything Shane never had a chance to be, just as he never had the opportunity to be Shane—although, who knows, he may have been before I was born—but had outlived that role.

And to the New Home of the Novella Form: Spout Hill Press.

Acknowledgements

To Ruth Francisco of *Venice West Review*, who wanted to publish this novella, but wasn't quite able to.

Foreward

That which we love we make sacred.

I think this is true.

Follow me through this thought process because I might be off base here. We sanctify romance through marriage and children through baptism.

That's how we used to do it anyway.

We sanctify (or sanctified) the love of our gods with ceremonies and communion and our love of country with ceremonies and pledges.

The thing is we haven't lost our loves, but we have lost the idea of the sacred. We've lost that mechanism to point to things and say, "This is so beautiful God loves it."

Or I should say that many of us have lost that.

How then do we point to the thing that we love and elevate it above the rest when we've lost that mechanism to make it holy?

Gerald Locklin writes about it.

And his novella, *Come Back Bear*, is an homage to so many things, but it has taken American popular cultural icons and has raised them to mythological significance. For to him and for so many of us, *Shane* is the mythology of our lives. We understood who we were as children in reaction to that great novel. We understand what it means to be adults when we reread it years later.

Shane is of course the great centerpiece of Locklin's work, but it is not the only thing that has become holy. So has the desert Southwest and fellow western writers and the bond between a father and his children. So have so many things.

In the end, he is pointing to America and saying that it is sacred.

At least, I think that's true.

--John Brantingham,
author of *Let Us All Pray
Now to Our Own
Strange Gods*

Come Back, Bear

The kid walked into my office and said, "Come back, Shane."

I looked up from my sports section in which I had been reading about the California Cherubs' 3986th consecutive loss. They were threatening to break their own record.

"Yeah, kid," I said, "it's a great movie, my personal favorite—in fact, I consider it the high point of Western Art, in which I do not include just Oaters, but all those yawners like *Oedipus* and *King Lear* and *An American Tragedy*—but the sorry fact remains that I ain't Shane, not by a long shot."

"What is your name?" the kid asked.

"Well," I answered, "I could get real artsy with you and tell you, My name is Shame or *Skammen*, as we say it at the *It's-in-the-Cannes Film Festival*, but the fact is, My Name is Bear."

"*Bear*," the kid mused, "I guess that *Bear* will do as long as you're a First-Rate Full-Time Gunfighter."

"Listen, kid," I said, "I'm First-Rate at everything I do…*but I'm only an occasional* Gunfighter. Most of the time I'm a Dick. And I'm not just Any Old Dick, let alone Any Old Tom and Harry. I'm not just One More First-Rate Dick. I'm The Best Dick. But luckily for you, when properly

3

motivated, I can at a moment's notice slip into the role of Gunfighter. And when I slip into the role of Gunfighter I become not just Any Old Gunfighter—I become The Best Gunfighter."

"Then you'll come back with me?"

"Wait a minute," I said, "I'm afraid I do not exactly feel properly motivated."

"How's this for motivation," the kid said, and he shined a fist at me. I was momentarily blinded.

"Jesus Christ," I said, "what is it?"

"The Gold Ring."

"*The* Gold Ring?"

"*The* Gold Ring."

"Where'd you get it?"

"From my mother. Incidentally, she's part of the bargain."

"What?"

"You get to fuck my mother."

"No shit. Is she good looking?"

"She's the best-looking woman in town. Of course she's also the only woman in town. But she's also better looking than any of the sheep, and one of those furry devils—the best looking one—just happens to be wearing my high-school ring. *Flossie*, her name is."

4

I Don The Garb Of A Gunfighter

"Okay," I told the kid, "you've made me an offer that I could easily refuse if I had any other offers, but I haven't had any other offers in about fifteen years, so I guess I will graciously accept yours."

I was attired in the garb of a Dick. A Very Private Dick. They were not, unfortunately, the togs of a dick who is regularly employed, but those of a dick who has not had a case in fifteen years.

A shirt, pants, socks, shoes. A threadbare sports coat draped over the back of a chair. A .45 in a holster hanging from a closet doorknob.

No gold chains.

"I guess I better get me some gunfighter duds," I told the kid.

"You damn well better get yourself something," the kid replied.

The Earl Shoop Memorial Duds-for-Dudes Store

We piled into my rotting white Toyota station wagon and hopped on the freeway for Hollywood. I turned off on Hollywood Boulevard and cruised to a little place near Cahuenga known as the Earl Shoop Memorial Duds-for-Dudes Store. The kid said, "Who was Earl Shoop?"

"Oh, he was a character in a Nathanael West novel entitled *The Day of the Locust*. He was an out-of-work Hollywood extra, a big dumb guy whose claim to fame is that a dwarf once swung from his balls."

"Doesn't take much to get something named after you in this town, does it?"

"I don't know," I said, "you ever know anyone else who had a dwarf swing from his balls?"

"I guess not," the kid said, "but what the heck, I'm just a kid. For all I know it may be a daily occurrence around these parts."

The Old Three-Gun Theory

I traded in my .38 on a Colt .45 with an ivory handle.

"Maybe you ought to git yourself two guns," the kid suggested.

"Didn't Shane always say a man only needs one gun if he knows how to use it?"

"That's right. Do you know how to use it?"

"Not very well. In fact, I think I'll git me *three* guns just to be certain."

I also traded in my Incognito Dick outfit on a blue work shirt and a buckskin jacket and boots and spurs.

I had to take an eleven-gallon hat because the ten-gallon hats wouldn't fit my head. Too many years of being pistol whipped and slapped, I guess, although it certainly had not affected my intelligence.

I strode to the swinging doors in my new gunfighter duds, my three guns in three different holster-belts strapped around my waist. I slammed my way through and clicked onto the boulevard sidewalk with my thumbs locked in two of my belts. I could really have used an extra thumb.

"Come back, Bear!"

I knew I was cutting one hell of an impressive figure because all traffic—motorized and ambulatory—had jarred to a halt. All eyes were on me. Even the pigeons seemed curious.

"Come back, Bear! Come back inside!"

"Shut up, kid; you're spoiling the effect."

"Please, Bear!"

"What in the world is the matter with you, kid?"

"The pants, Bear. You forgot to buy any pants."

I gazed down at my white, hairless legs.

I backed into the store.

The Old One-Chap Theory

They only had one chap left.

They had just sold all the rest to a troupe of 35 riders from a one-legged rodeo.

I figured one chap was better than none.

I took it.

The salesman also sold me a case of chapsticks to keep the chap from getting dry and raw.

A Bevy Of Immortals

It was uncomfortable driving my white Toyota wagon wearing spurs, but a gunfighter must make sacrifices.

A crowd was milling about the courtyard of Grauman's Chinese Theatre. I slowed and rolled down my window. A stunning older woman was hurrying past: "Say, aren't you…"

"Catherine Sideburn. Yes."

"And isn't that…"

"Yes. Helene Schleyes."

"And that third handsome old doll is…"

"Mary Barton. Still pixieish, not sixtyish."

"And where are you hurrying to?"

"Juan (The Rod) Soames is having his dick-print immortalized in cement."

"Dick? But *I'm* the Best Dick!"

"You?! Delusions of Grandeur are rampant in this town."

And the three great ladies of the American Theatre hurried on.

"C'mon," I said to the kid, "I want to see this."

We had trouble wedging our way through the crowd. When we got to a clearing, Juan (The Rod) Soames was supporting himself naked on his fingers and toes and lowering his erect clam-digger towards the rectangle of cement.

"Doesn't look like such a great dick to me," I huffed, but at that very moment, I was shoved forward, stepped on a teenager's surfboard, and landed in a somersault supine on the hard surface. One of my three six-shooters discharged, the bullet grazing Juan (The Rod) Soames' left buttock. He lunged forward and landed splat on the wet patch of cement. He tried to rise but cried out, "I can't budge! I'm stuck! What is this stuff?"

"Oh my God," the theatre manager exclaimed, "could the maintenance men have gotten the instant-stick airplane solution by mistake?"

I was myself more successful at standing, but only to find myself a split-second later sliding on a spilled Orange Julius. I was once again airborne and this time all three guns exploded upon landing, setting off a molecule-like ricocheting.

Three silver-tressed matrons clutched their hearts and sank to the ground.

The kid said, "Yikes, let's split this place—you've just retired *les trois grandes dames* of the American Theatre."

I ran for the station wagon, but caught my spurs while hurdling a low chain fence. Only two of the pistols discharged this time, but I saw a couple just emerging from a sports car drop in pain.

"Jesus Christ, Bear," the kid said, "that was Paul Moonman and Joanne Greensward." And I read in today's paper that they were only one day short of celebrating their 100th wedding anniversary. The longest other Hollywood marriage on record was just fifty-six days. I really think it would behoove us to get out of this place."

Big Bear or Bust

We took the Hollywood to the San Bernardino Freeway and an hour later I turned off at Redlands and started to wind my way up Highway 38 in the shadow of Mt. San Gorgonio.

"Hey, where we goin'?"

"Big Bear."

"I thought *you* were the Big Bear."

"I am."

"You mean this place was named after you?"

I decided not to answer him. No harm in letting him think whatever he wanted to.

Beer and Birria

In the foothills above Redlands, just before you start up into the canyon proper, is a town called Mentone Beach. Mentone Beach is about seventy-five miles from the nearest ocean, but I guess the name of the place has something to do with the mentalities of at least some of the inhabitants, their lifestyles, perhaps their chemical preferences.

I pulled into a place called Juan's Place. I said to the kid, "Let's have a taco and an enchilada."

The kid said, "I thought you'd never ask."

We ate in the bar. Juan's specialties are goat tacos and enchiladas made with the sort of white cheese implicated in the epidemic in which seventy-five people died last summer. But they were mostly pregnant women and new mothers. I never miss a chance to partake of the *specialités* of Juan's cuisine. Besides, a beer never tastes better than when you're washing down one of Juan's goat tacos with it.

Halfway through the light repast, the kid said, "Can I have some of your beer? I've been chewing on this first bite of goat taco for about seven minutes now and I don't think I'll ever manage to swallow it without a swig of beer."

"Sure, kid," I said, "you're a little young still but Juan never minds a young man having a beer with his surrogate father."

14

I poured half the beer into a glass and pushed it toward the kid, while keeping the bottle for myself. The kid swallowed a big gulp of beer and *birria* and sighed with relief. A split-second later the beer glass shattered in his hand. Smoke was curling towards the ceiling from a pistol in the hand of Juan Mentonita. Juan's holster was strapped over a dingy white apron that could have served as a canopy for an outdoor stadium.

"Can't you guys read?" Juan asked and pointed at the wall. I don't know how I could have missed the sign at which he was pointing:

NO DRINKING BY YOUNG TURKS
EVEN IF (OR ESPECIALLY IF)
IN THE COMPANY OF SURROGATE FATHERS
VIOLATORS WILL BE SHOT

"Sorry, Bear," Juan said, "but I'm gonna have to shoot the kid."

"Fair enough, Juan," I said, "he broke the law, and if you let one young whippersnapper break the law, pretty soon every young whippersnapper in town will be thinking that he can get away with it too. Son, prepare your soul to meet its maker. And finish your goddamn food. Think about all the starving Indochinese kids in Garden Grove."

"Okay," the kid said, "but pass the *salsa*."

I passed him the little dishes of salsa verde and salsa Colorado and he deftly flipped the first into Juan's right eye and the second into his left. "Ay-yiii-yiii-yiiiii!" exclaimed Juan. "Cielito lindo! La Cucaracha! Mi casa es su casa! Cuando caliente el sol!"

The kid disappeared cooly into the kitchen and returned with the carcass of a goat with which he proceeded to pound Juan methodically into submission.

The eyes of the other customers grew wide as chiles rellenos as they whispered in unison, "Ay caramba!"

The kid stopped beating a rosy tattoo on Juan's male pattern baldness and asked, "Do I have to eat everything on my plate?"

I heard sirens in the distance.

"I guess not," I said, "but don't tell me you're hungry as soon as we're back on the road."

A Little Bit Of Growing Up

We were no sooner back on the road than the kid said, "I'm hungry."

"Well," I said, displaying my world-renowned disciplining skills, "I guess we could stop for root-beer floats at the A&W stand. It's almost a ritual."

The root-beer floats were more than just great—they were both hermeneutically and psychoanalytically significant. We emerged from the A&W stand cosmically refreshed...only to find our path to the station wagon blocked by eighteen leather-jacketed members of the Hogs-For-Christ motorcycle gang.

"What's this all about?" I said.

"We want the kid," their spokesman said. He was a twerp who no doubt had nothing to contribute to the gang except his spokesmanship. "Just give us the kid and you can go your own way."

"What do you want the kid for?"

"We want to take him up the hill and fuck him in the ass. It's nothing personal. It's just a sort of ritual."

"Oh," I said, "a ritual. Yeah, I guess that makes it okay. But first let me ask you one question. It's just a sort of ritual of my own."

"Go ahead."

"What was your major?"

"My major?"

"Yeah. In college. What did you major in, in college?"

"Try to guess. Three guesses."

"And if I guess correctly, then you guys will leave the kid alone?"

"Sure, sport."

"Screenwriting."

"How did you know that?"

"I guessed it, didn't I? On my first try. I didn't even need my two other guesses."

"*How did you know?*"

"Because you seem to think you can improve on the original."

"You're a dead man, Daddy-o. If you hadn't been a wise-ass, you could have walked. But now we kill you first and then we fuck the kid."

I drew two of my three six-shooters and pumped bullets into the hearts of twelve of the eighteen bikers. I knew the remaining six would drill us, but I wanted to go down with the satisfaction of having taken as many as possible with me.

To my slack-jawed surprise, all eighteen went down clutching their chests.

The kid had drawn my other gun. He had crouched in the arc of my widened stance and unloaded the cylinders into the middle six villains as I had dispatched those to the left and the right.

"Not bad shooting for a kid, kid," I said.

The Bad Guys Are Back

"Well," the kid said, "it looks like the bad guys are back."

"As if," I said.

"As if what?" he said.

"Correct your grammar," I said, "it looks *as if* the bad guys are back. *Like* is a preposition not a conjunction."

"You're a very old-fashioned grammarian," the kid said.

"That's right," I said, "I'm a very old-fashioned grammarian and I used to be a very old-fashioned dick and now I am a very old-fashioned gunfighter. But yes, you're right—the bad guys are back. The bad guys always return like cockroaches and bad pennies. And notice my correct use of the preposition *like*."

A Sociological Dialogue

"What do you suppose accounts for the rather constant presence of bad guys in the literature and life of the Western World? Is capital to blame?"

"I don't know. Maybe partly."

"Does it have anything to do with Jung's archetypes of the collective unconscious?"

"I don't know. Maybe partly."

"Does it have anything to do with the conditions of our prisons?"

"They certainly don't seem to be making things better."

"How about The American Family?"

"What American family?"

"Are you in favor of the death penalty?"

"I figure anyone who votes for it is no more and no less guilty of killing than you and I were back there with the eighteen bikers. Except that we had balls enough to do the killing ourselves."

"What about nutrition?"

"Almost every juvenile admitted to juvenile hall is found to be suffering from malnutrition."

"What about drugs?"

"I drink."

"What about other drugs?"

"I've seen them do incredible harm on an incredible scale."

"Then you're for mandatory drug testing, lie detector tests and such."

"No, I am adamantly opposed to all such incursions upon civil liberties. In fact I am one of the only dicks/gunfighters who is a dues-paying member of the American Civil Liberties Union. Although I'll admit to having violated a few civil liberties in my day."

"Then could you give us one last word on your Theory of Bad Guys?"

"I don't know what causes them. I am willing to work in any reasonable way to alleviate any likely causes of Bad-Guyism. But in the meantime it's just my job to deal with them."

Billy Jack's Woman

Passing a meadow, I heard what seemed to be sounds of violence and resistance. I pulled the Toyota onto a fireroad and raced into the center of the valley. There a reasonably attractive though somewhat washed-out woman lay spread-eagled on her back, her wrists and ankles bound to four wooden stakes. She was stark naked.

"Thank God," she said, "you've scared them off!"

"Scared whom off?"

"Billy's enemies. The enemies of the school."

"What were they doing?"

"I think it's fairly obvious what they were *trying* to do. Serendipitously you arrived just in the nick of time. Now untie me, please."

The kid went to untie her.

"Wait a minute, kid," I said; "What's the big hurry?"

"For Christ's sake, Bear, the woman is suffering. And Billy Jack is one of my super-heroes. Yours too, I bet. How can there be any question of where our duty lies?"

"But look," I said, "how often are we apt to fall into a chance like this?"

"I can't believe this," Jeanie said.

"The kid said, "I can't believe it either."

"Look," I said, "I'm not suggesting that we torture her or humiliate her or even that we necessarily fuck her. But before we let her go, what would be the big harm in our just playing around a little bit?"

For the flicker of a second, I thought I perceived the kid weakening, but at just that moment Jeanie demanded, "Young man, what would your mother think if she could see you now?"

"Oh fuck," the kid said, "I forgot all about Mom," and freed Jeanie posthaste from her thongs.

"You snake," she spat at me; you slime."

"C'mon," I said, "you didn't think I was *serious*, did you? Why I was just conducting a little moral survey on the youth of today."

"You're no mythic gunfighter," she said, "you're a real one. Now get the fuck out of this legendary valley before Billy Jack gets back from National Guard drills and kicks you upside both your temples."

A Post-Deconstructive Train Of Thought

Out of nowhere, the kid asked me, "Are we trapped in a metafictional novel?"

(Well, maybe it wasn't out of nowhere. Maybe it had something to do with the paperback copy of Patricia Waugh's *Metafiction* that he had just looked up from.)

"No," I said, "we are trapped in a meta-metafictional novel. Also, I think our author has, along with a lot of unsavory personality traits, a deeply rooted love of westerns. Maybe even an almost sick need for them."

"But who," the kid said, "can draw the fine line where love ends and mental illness begins?"

"I can," I said.

How Can Anyone Bring Kids Into Our World?

"You have kids, don't you, Bear? I mean kids even beyond me?"

"Yes," I said.

"How can you justify bringing kids into our modern twentieth century world of today?"

"Listen, kid," I said," my grandmother had fourteen kids and lost five of them in a single week in 1918 to an influenza outbreak. Today my kids get the flu and they go to bed for a couple of days and then they go back to school."

"Then what you are saying is that in spite of the threat of nuclear and ecological annihilation that you don't think our world is horribly worse than places/times of the past?"

"I wasn't there, kid," I said, "but I really kind of doubt it."

State-Of-The-Art Bad Guy Study

Before settling into the cabin in the valley, we stopped to pick up a couple of six-packs and a newspaper. On the front page of the newspaper was an article about a study purporting to prove that nearly all bad guys show evidence of some degree of brain damage. The brain damage, however, was not usually sufficient in itself to cause aggressive behavior. It generally had to be accompanied by a history of abuse as a child and that abuse did not necessarily have to be physical but could be the culmination of severe and unrelenting criticism.

The kid said, "What do you think, Bear?"

"Hell, what do I know? I suspect they may be right, at least to a great extent. It's a pleasant surprise, at least, to find someone still looking for causes and cures instead of crueler and more unusual forms of punishment. On the other hand I hope the study isn't used to justify some sort of preventive custody. Or surgery, for that matter."

"Bear," the kid said, "how far do you figure you and I are from being just like the bad guys?"

"Kid," I said, "there but for the grace of God go all of us."

An Introduction

It was beginning to get dark. "Bear," the kid said, "how much farther is it to the cabin?"

"We just passed the turn-off," I said. "I decided to take you into town and introduce you to a friend of mine."

All but a couple of regulars had drifted away from The Large-Mouthed Bass Bar and Fish Joint. Big Hilda was behind the bar, chatting with the old-timers. They were discussing The Big One. The Big One had reportedly been spotted once again, flinging itself into the air from the snow-cold waters of Jenks Lake. The Big One had reportedly stared this holidaying truck driver in the eye and challenged, "Come and get me, Fatso." There was a lot of disagreement over the precise species that The Big One represented, but it was unanimously agreed hereabouts that The Big One could talk.

When Big Hilda wandered down to our end of the bar, I said, "Hilda, I'd like you to meet the kid."

"Pleased to meet you, young man," Hilda said, taking the kid's hand and holding it longer than necessary. She was wearing a dirndl, and the kid was staring desperately into her cleavage.

"What will the young gentleman have?" Big Hilda asked.

28

"Give him a Jägermeister with a Ritterbrau back," I said.

"Jah," Big Hilda said. "Is *gut*."

The last couple pushed back their stools and prepared to leave. "Hilda," I said, "I was thinking of running into town to collect a little gambling debt from Wee Willie Winkie at the Silver Slalom. Do you think you could babysit the kid here until I get back?"

"Yah, sure," she said. "He is a *gut* boy, dot is plain to see. I will be locking the door behind you now, and he can just sit here and drinken der schnapps and der beer and der keepen me company while I do my closing chores."

"But Bear," the kid protested, "what if you encounter trouble while attempting to collect your gambling debt?"

"It'll be okay, kid," I said. "Wee Willie Winkie is very wee indeed. Isn't that right, Big Hilda?"

Hilda looked up from her broom long enough to say, "Yah, Wee Willie Winkie he ist der wee-wee-est. Not like this big strong strapping gentleman friend of mine here." And she gave the kid a squeeze on the bicep that made him go red in the face. Hilda herself must have been getting in some water-skiing because she was as golden as a Mama Bear.

"Give the kid another round and put it on my tab," I said, "and I'll see you both when I see you."

The Night

Of course there was no gambling debt to collect. I don't win bets, I lose them and so I try not to gamble any more than is absolutely necessary to the maintaining of an image.

I drove back to the Ranch Lake Road and let the Toyota creep over the dust and rocks to the gambrel in the center of the valley. I left the car lights on until I had gotten the front door unlocked. Then I moved into the house the few necessities, locked the car, and locked myself inside the cabin.

I turned off all the lights and felt my way upstairs to the northwest-facing bedroom. I took off all my clothes and lay them on the bed. Then I slid back the glass door of the porch and walked out onto it.

It was total darkness except for the moon and Ursa Major and the planets. It was total silence except for the always powerful wind and the tragicomic mating calls of the wild burros. I stood there for a long time in the silent darkness not trying to put my thoughts into words, not even trying to think. Then I came inside and lay down on the bed.

I dreamed I was in snow-covered mountains in Colorado, maybe Independence Pass, and I was trying to make a trek before dark with my woman and my children. A nameless, faceless friend was with us and a little ways up the trail we met two of his enemies. One of them set upon him and beat him vividly, with the awful collision of human bone on bone that is so sickeningly real in life, as opposed to even the bloodiest of scenes on a screen. By the time the second enemy could intervene, our friend was either dead or so close to it that were he to survive he would never resemble the man that he had been.

I think he kept up with us for a while and then fell back.

Through this my only instinct had been to keep my woman and children and myself out of the violence.

We had a head start on the enemies and while they never seemed to gain any ground on us, then never seemed to lose any either.

The snow grew deeper. A slippery crust was beginning to form on it. There was a danger of sliding down the crest and off the side of the mountain. I did not seem to be able to convince my children of the lethal danger of this. There was that horrible moment where you are almost tempted to cry out at them… "All right then, go ahead, kill yourself, see what I care,"… and then you are filled with dread and the shame that you could ever even have thought such a thing.

It became apparent that the road across the mountains and the road back were both going to be closed for the night. All the shelters were filling up quickly. Like Joseph, I had to find a lean-to for my family for the night...

Then I was awake in the darkness and the silence was being broken by a voice that said, "Nothing is lost... since before the Indians, since as far back as forever nothing has been lost that cannot be retrieved."

Shaking, I got out of bed, went down the stairs to the kitchen, and poured myself a drink. Then another. Then a third. I am not as great an alcoholic as the other kid, that grown-up kid, Kid Shaleen, but I do find a drink to be a comfort on occasion. The trick on this transfigured night was to know just how much would let me sleep without leaving me sick in the morning.

A Bittersweet Awakening

I awoke to a lovely smell that I could barely recollect, that of bacon frying and a pot of hot coffee on the fire. In the kitchen I found the kid at work in front of the stove. He looked more refreshed than exhausted.

"Miss Hilda dropped me off," he smiled.

"You get your money?"

"Oh yes. You have a good time with Big Hilda?"

"A wonderful time," he said. "Miss Hilda is a wonderful woman," ... and then he began to frown ... "Bear, would you tell me something?"

"Sure."

"Did you ever ... I mean, when you were a young man, did you ever ... you know ... with Miss Hilda?"

"No," I said, wondering how different my life might have turned out if I had.

"You wouldn't ever ... you know ... *now*, would you?"

"No, kid," I said, "Miss Hilda is a fine woman, but I wouldn't make advances to her unless I was sure you were yourself no longer interested."

"Well, don't ever assume I'm not unless I tell you so, okay?"

"Okay," I said. "I won't come on to her even if you do say that you're over her, because you may just be trying to convince yourself."

"Thanks, Bear," he said.

I went into the bathroom then, and beneath the roar of the shower stream I touched myself to visions of the warm and supple comforts of Big Hilda, who was never to be mine again.

The Great Frozen Burrito Massacre

"Bear, Bear, come quick!"

"What is it, son?"

"They're gunning down the wild burros. They're gunning them down to make them into frozen burritos."

I strapped on my three gun belts and strode outside. Sure enough, it was the idiots in the three-wheeled off-road vehicles who were not only stirring up the dust and decibels, but who were also gunning down the burros, Buffalo Bill style. A platoon of roach coaches were darting in and out of the fallen, protected animals, scooping them up and processing them, almost on the hoof, into frozen burritos.

"Did you reload my pistols, son?" I asked.

"Yes, sir," the kid replied, "and I even tinkered with them a bit in the interests of efficiency."

"Jesus Christ," I said, "I sure hope you didn't fuck them up."

We bumped the Toyota out into the middle of the slaughter then. There were more than eighteen of them this time, that was for sure, and they were armed with everything from machine guns to bazookas.

"You drive, kid," I said, "and as soon as we switched seats I rolled down the window, extended two pistols, and began gunning down violators of the state game laws. When I had emptied three barrels of eighteen cartridges, I thought we were doomed, but the kid said, "I told you I tinkered a bit with the weapons. Just spin the barrels and try again."

I spun the barrels and sure enough they were reloaded.

"Where the hell did you learn that trick?" I asked the kid.

"Trade Tech," he replied, "and not in the classroom."

Going After The Big One

We closed the cabin back up then, repacked the car, and started up over Onyx Summit and back down the mountain. The kid asked, "Are we going to go save Ma now?"

"Not yet."

"Then where are we going?"

"We are going after The Big One."

The Big One Speaks To Us

I pulled onto the upper road to Jenks Lake and wound back in through the forest. It was the time of day when fishermen's lore has it that the fish are napping and just as I had hoped, there was no one else along the shore.

The Big One, of course, was taking no siesta. I cast out to the deepest pool and a moment later The Big One came flying into the air, the barb of my lure through his lip. He hung in mid-air and said, "Where did you learn to tie The Magic Fly?"

"From my father, who learned from his father, who learned from his father, who learned from his father."

"And will you teach this kid?"

"When the time comes. If he wishes."

"Okay. You know the rules. For my freedom I grant you the answer to one question."

"My question is, *What is your name*?"

"My name is *Trout Fishing in America*."

And at that The Big One was freed from the hook and fell back into the once-glacial depths.

"What was that all about?" the kid asked.

"That, my son, was a tribute to a Great American Writer."

A Born-Again Real Estate Baron

"That was a nice cabin," the kid said. "How long you had it?"

"Less than a year. It was the first thing I ever bought on credit in my life. I've always paid cash for second-hand cars and I've lived in apartments ever since leaving home. So my wife and I were always getting slaughtered at tax time. The cabin helped a little this year but, you know, you never stop paying bills for utilities and repairs. And at that altitude things are always freezing and cracking and leaking and warping. It's sure been a crash course in real estate, though."

"Would you do it over?"

"Oh sure. In fact, now that I've gotten a taste of ownership, I'd like to buy up that double-lot on the left with the big tree on it. And then the lot in back so that no one can build right up on top of us. Gradually, to tell you the truth, I'd like to buy up the entire valley, then the entire mountain, and then I'd get started on some other nice place like Julian or Idyllwild."

"Once you owned all the mountains in Southern California, what would you do with them?"

"*Do* with them? Why I wouldn't do anything with them. I'd just *own* them."

"And what if poor people came along, immigrants maybe, farmers, and wanted to squat on your land?"

"Well, they wouldn't have any right to do that because it would be *my land.*"

"But what if they did it anyway?"

"Why I'd ask them nicely to get off my land and then if they didn't I'd have to get the sheriff to evict them."

"And what if they still wouldn't go?"

"Then I guess I'd have to burn their barns down. And if that didn't work I'd burn their homes. If necessary I'd shoot one or two of them and as a last resort I'd kill them all."

"Dad, don't you see the forces you're identifying with? Don't you realize that you're falling into the trap of private property that turns a good man into one of the bad guys? Didn't you ever see *Heaven's Gate*? *Shane*? Didn't you read *Bury My Heart at Wounded Knee*? Or *The Bear*?"

"Oh yeah, I loved all of them. But they weren't set in *my* valley."

What Is It About Dinosaurs?

"Aren't we going south?"

"We're going just a little south."

"But we have to go north to see Mom!"

"I know, kid. We'll head north all in our own good time. First I want you to see a couple of dinosaurs."

"Dinosaurs?"

"Sure, don't you like dinosaurs? I thought all kids loved dinosaurs."

"All *little* kids love dinosaurs, Bear. When I was a *little* kid I was *crazy* about dinosaurs. But I'm not a little kid any more. I'm a *big* kid whose mother's life and virtue is under siege. So frankly, just as this particular moment, I don't really give a flying fuck about dinosaurs!"

"Well, I want to pick up a couple of souvenirs for my own little boy and girl then."

Dinosaurs Are Free

I pulled onto the gravel in front of the
dinosaurs out at the truckstop on Highway 10 that
are in innumerable films of the Sam Shepard ilk.
We trudged inside of the brontosaurus and up the
stairs to the gift shop. I picked out a set of dinosaur
toys and asked the old man behind the counter how
much they were. He said, "Ten dollars."

"That's highway robbery," I said.

"Take it or leave it, weirdo," said the old
fuck.

"C'mon, kid," I said, and we trudged back out
to the car where I proceeded to strap on the three
gun belts. "Jesus, Bear," the kid said, "don't do it.
I'll give you the lousy ten bucks."

"Stay here, kid," I said; "warm up the
engine."

"Bear," the kid said, "we're in the middle of
the goddamn desert. The car is practically boiling
over."

"Keep me covered, kid," I said, and I walked
tall towards the dinosaur. Once up the stairs, I drew
one of my three guns and said, "Hand over all the
dinosaur toys in the place."

The old gent didn't waste any time loading up
my free arm with dinosaur toys. The ones I couldn't
handle, he carried out to the Toyota himself. We

piled the shopful of dinosaur toys into the back of the station wagon.

"This is highway robbery," complained the elderly gentleman.

"Don't steal my lines," I said, and we started north until he ran back into the brontosaurus. Then we hung a u-ie and continued towards the Great Southwest.

Parking at a bar outside of Indio, I said to the kid, "Let's have a beer. I have an account to settle in this place."

"Another gambling debt?"

"In a manner of speaking. Except the fellow didn't know that he was risking anything."

We entered the barroom. There were a bunch of California cowboys at the bar who turned to give us the once-over. At the sight of my single chap, a sneer began to form over their noble rustic countenances. I walked up to the tallest and the grizzliest and delivered a high swift knee to the groin. Spinning like a Shiva I sliced the heel of a blade-like hand into his Adam's apple. The kid had drawn two of my guns which were more than enough to keep a drop on the other customers. To the bartender, I said, "Let's get some olives from the storeroom. In fact, let's get *all* the olives from the storeroom.

"Olives?"

"You heard me."

We carried all the cases of ten-pound jars of olives into the barroom then and I invited the customers to start partaking of my repast. I told the bartender to let them have all the refills of beer they needed with which to wash down the olives. And since the big, bad Strothers surrogate was starting to breathe a little easier now, I slammed his face into an open jar of olives also.

One of the boys at the bar took his face out of the trough long enough to ask, "How many olives do we have to eat?"

"All of them," I said.

"That's impossible."

"Then you better enjoy your meal, because if a single olive is left by midnight, then this is your Last Supper."

I didn't hold them to that, of course. I only made them eat until they were all deathly ill, rolling into each other on the floor and puking upon each other a green slime of beer and half-digested olives. Then I said, "Boys, I was in this bar once many years ago. I was on a trip to Tucson with my two youngest children of that era, mere babes, and I brought them in here for a hotdog and coke and to use the restroom. And either because I looked a little weird to you, or maybe in those days a little straight, or maybe because I ordered a dark imported beer, Shit-for-Brains here saw to it that my beer glass arrived with an olive in it. And the rest of you stood around and near-to-yukked yourselves to death. And because I had to think first of the safety of my kids, and because it was in every way a low period in my life, and because I was so hungover that day that I could hardly swallow my beer without spilling it, I had to pretend not to notice the immensely humorous olive. Well, now you know that I did notice it, so enjoy the culmination of your comic brainstorm, gentlemen. Enjoy yourselves once again at my expense."

Gila Bend

We came to Gila Bend and the kid asked, "Do you believe in Gila monsters?"

"Of course I believe in Gila monsters. Gila monsters are a natural, not a supernatural phenomenon.

"Have you ever seen a Gila monster?"

"Yes, of course I have."

"Where did you see it?"

"I saw it in the motion picture version of *The Treasure of the Sierra Madre*."

"Do you believe they don't unclench their jaws from you even after they're dead?"

"Why wouldn't I believe it? It just puts them in the same class with human beings."

A Family Man

"Bear," the kid said, "didn't you mention having a wife and kids?"

"Yes. Definitely."

"Did it occur to you to let them know you were going on this trip?"

"Oh my God, I completely forgot to call home."

"Well, maybe you ought to do so right now."

"You're right, kid; you're absolutely right."

So we took a cheap motel in Gila Bend, Arizona, and the kid went to catch a few rays by the pool, and I went in search of a pay phone. I found one behind the Pizza Hut that was situated between Bill Cody's coin shop and Sitting Bull's rock shop. My daughter answered the phone:

"Hi sweetheart, how was school today?"

"It was fine. I love school."

"How were your piano and dancing lessons?"

"They were fine."

"I miss you terribly."

"I miss you terribly too. Did you have to go away?"

"Yes. I think so. I don't know. Where's your mother?"

"She's in the bedroom sulking."

"Does she miss me?"

"Well, not exactly. Actually, she just says that you don't have enough life insurance. Will you be home soon?"

"Just as soon as possible."

"My brother would like to talk to you."

"Fine. Put him on … Hi, big guy …"

"Daddy?"

"Yes?"

"Can you bring us some dinosaur toys?"

"You know, old guy, dinosaur toys are really hard to come by out here in the Great American West, but I'll do my best … I just might be able to arrange it."

The Kid

When I returned to the pool there was a young girl lying by it, a slender thing just on the cusp between girlhood and young womanhood. I asked her, "Seen a kid around here?"

"I am the kid now, Bear. Is that okay?"

"You're the kid? Why, yes, sure it's okay. Pleased to meetcha, kid. But what happened?"

"I dove into the pool a boy and I climbed out a girl. It must be a magic pool. Do you mind?"

"No, I don't mind … but I'm sure as fuck going to stay my distance from that magic pool."

That night we dined on the regional cuisine, a Triple Jalapeno Gila Hopalong Cassidy at the Pizza Hut. And I asked the kid, "Does our mission remain unchanged?"

"Oh yes."

"And you're sure your mother will recognize you?"

"Oh yes."

"Well, I guess there ain't much point in turning back at this stage of the chase."

Loyal Opposition

In the middle of the Sonora Desert we came upon a military exercise reminiscent of Rommel in North Africa. "Are we on an army base?" the kid gasped.

"No," I said, "these people are all civilians, although some of them may have been in the military at one time and some of them may be off-duty cops."

"What are they doing?"

"They're practicing overthrowing the government."

"Why do they want to do that?"

"I guess they've convinced themselves that the government has been (or soon will be) taken over by The Blacks or The Jews or The Commies or The Gays or The ACLU or The Rockefellers or The Trilateral Commission or some combination of the above."

"Aren't you going to do something about them?"

"What can I do?"

"Cripes, Bear, I thought you were kind of like a Superman or something. I mean, I thought you could take care of anything that needed taking care of."

"Well, I can't. And even if I could do something, what *should* I do? Murder the lot of them? Assassinate their leaders? Make of them the martyrs and victims of persecution that in their own imaginations they already are?"

"Could you at least make them all eat a few jars of olives?"

"That would be fun, kid, but just a trifle self-indulgent. I'll tell you what: if I ever find anyone being victimized by them, I'll do my best to intervene. And if a civil war ever does break out, I'll be on no side at all before I'll be on their side. And if they should happen to get raided by the police today for weapons violations, I'll enjoy the heck out of seeing them on the late news."

"You could stop at the next pay phone and blow the whistle on them."

"Not my style, kid. And anyway, do they look like they're worried a whole helluva lot about the police?"

Trivia Question: Who Played the Eighth Samurai?

At the junction of the Nogales Highway we waited while seven horsemen clunked past. The kid's jaw dropped: "Bear, aren't those …"

"Sure are." And she was even impressed when the horseman riding lead caught my eye and, with a grin of recognition, shouted, "Bear, c'mon and join us!"

"To Mexico? It's too hot this time of year."

"Wouldn't you like to alleviate a little injustice?"

"Sure. But I don't have to go to Mexico to find injustice. I don't even have to go to Mexico to find Mexicans."

"There may be gold in it."

"There may be a bullet hole in it. Besides, I've seen *The Treasure of the Sierra Madre* enough times to have learned that gold is more deadly than Gila monsters."

"You're not getting yellow, are you? Yellow like the ribbon in your little whore's hair?"

I started out of the Toyota and seven guns came out of their holsters. That was four more than my own.

"It's all right, Bear," the kid said. "Get back in the car before you get yourself killed and me gang-banged. Besides, they're just rough men who think they have to talk that way. I didn't even take it personally and you shouldn't either."

I got back into the car and the seven fired their guns into the air and rode on.

I did get one modicum of revenge, though. When I had the Toyota all ready to roll, I leaned out the window on the passenger's side and shot the two old mules that were pulling the wagon that was loaded with their booze.

Then I hauled ass out of there.

P.S.

They were *very old mules*.
Honest.

Tucson

That evening, after the kid had hit the sack, I wandered out for a taste of the Tucson night life. The first tavern I moseyed into was frozen as a *tableau vivant*. All eyes were on a middle-aged guy seated at a table and the young Turk standing across from him.

"Isn't that Johnny Pico?" I asked.

"Yeah," I was told, "and he's just informed the young Turk that he has him covered with a gun beneath the table."

"Hey, young Turk," I shouted, "he's faking. I can see from here that he doesn't have a thing except his dick beneath the table, and that little thing just barely qualifies as a *pee*-shooter."

Actually I couldn't see beneath the table at all, but it was kind of like a busman's holiday being a spectator at a gunfight. The young Turk drew and since the old gunfighter had been faking that was the legendary date that Johnny Pico got the living fecal matter blasted out of him.

Later that evening at another tavern in another bar, the same young Turk called my bluff. I didn't have a gun aimed at his balls beneath the table either—I had three guns drawn on him. From the back, someone yelled, "He's faking. I can see from here there ain't nothing 'neath the table but his dick—and that little thing couldn't give a good stir to a whiskey soda."

The young Turk drew and I plastered his nuts all over a Neil Diamond poster. With my remaining gun I made a banana split of the dick of the loudmouth in the back.

I figured it was high time I got home to bed then, because I'd read that your chances of meeting a violent end in the days of the Wild West were no worse than today as long as you stayed out of bars.

The next day I took the kid to my favorite zoo, the Arizona-Sonora Desert Museum, and to the prolific movie set, Old Tucson. "Do you remember in *Death Wish*, kid, that Charles Bronson comes here to learn how to shoot?"

"Oh yeah!"

"Well, I was in graduate school with the guy who wrote *Death Wish*, Brian Garfield. He already had twenty-four books in print by the age of twenty-four. He had six books accepted on one Saturday. When the English department wouldn't accept a historical novel he'd written as a Master's Thesis, and which had already been accepted by Macmillan's , he tossed off a Thesis on Stephen Crane in a weekend. He told me he'd written his first novel in three days and he never allowed himself more than a week for anything in the pulp lines. He'd been the youngest writer ever accepted to the Western Writers of America. He always gave all the parties because he was the only one of us who had any money and he was just naturally a generous guy and a gentleman. I saw him on a talk show a few years back protesting the showing of *Death Wish* on t.v. because the novel had been anti-vigilante. But obviously the Bronson portrayal had touched, as they say, some chord of helplessness and wished-for potency in the American consciousness."

To Hell With The Obligatory Hades Chapter

The next day we drove into Cochise County, stopping at Boot Hill in Tombstone.

It's always kind of fun to read the epitaphs, but I can never remember them afterwards.

I looked around for a Golden Bough, but I didn't see anything except palo verde and gray mesquite, so I didn't get to make a descent to the underworld this time around.

Also

I didn't see any Golden Birds on any Golden Boughs so I didn't have any guest lecturers to bring back to my 20th Century Lit Class either.

The Rip-Off At The O.K. Corral

We paid our admission to the O.K. Corral but I can never keep the sides of that one straight even *with* a program. I mean, at least the Magnificent Seven and the Dalton Brothers and the Jameses are all on the same side. I felt I owed it to the kid to take her to the O.K. Corral but it gave me a headache, so afterwards I went next door to the fine wooden touristy saloon for a drink.

Bisbee

We proceeded farther south to the elegant old mining town of Bisbee, with its lavender open-pit mine and its classic hotel, The Copper Queen, and I associated the place with Richard Shelton who was still moonlighting here and not even sending out his poems yet when he was my mentor-teacher at the University of Arizona in 1961. Now he's as well-known as any poet in America, but still a perfect gentleman, and still running poetry workshops for the prisoners, and still in love with the desert.

And I associated Bisbee with William Eastlake with whom I'd had so many excellent conversations at the annual meeting of the Western Literature Association in Ft. Worth, when he was there to accept their Lifetime Achievement Award.

And I associated Bisbee with copper miners, once again being laid off, phased out, priced back, and generally fucked over.

One hundred years after the gunfighter had seen his era grind to a halt, the miner and the heavy-industry laborer were seeing their own obsolescence set like a scarlet striated smogset upon the painted plain that stretched from Bisbee to the power plants of the Douglas/Agua Prieta border.

Another Great Writer Of The Great Southwest

After a drink at the Douglas Hotel, I drove us
back an alternate route through the hill country of
Fort Huachuca and the high plains ranches of
Patagonia. "Gerry Haslam set a great story called
'The Daciano' here," I said.

"Bear," the kid said, "aren't you a little
embarrassed by all this blatant namedropping?"

"Yes," I said, "I am, but it's the only way I
can call attention to writers who have written of the
West much more authentically than I could ever
hope to."

"Okay," she said, "why don't you just get it
out of your system once and for all. Is there anyone,
for instance, who loves Tucson even more than you
do and who writes about it more knowledgably?"

"Yes, my friend Ron Koertge does. Also, he
gave me the moniker, *Bear*."

"Is there anyone else you want to mention?"

"Yes, I want to mention Gary Sposito, whom
I first met in Tucson when we were both graduate
students in 1961, and who would be a first-rate
creative writer were he not more importantly a
world-class physicist, and through him I met Gerald
Haslam who is the premiere author and scholar of
Western American Literature of our generation."

"Is that it?"

"Well, not entirely. I'd also like to mention that I am told that Larry McMurtry, Ken Kesey, and Tom McGuane all studied under Wallace Stegner at Stanford, the latter two simultaneously."

"Can we assume you at last are done dropping names?"

"Probably, but I can't absolutely guarantee it."

That night I took the kid out for two dinners at the world's two greatest Mexican restaurants (both very cheap) El Charro (downtown) and Taverna Karichimaka (Via Ajo Way and the road to the White Dove of the Desert—Mission San Xavier del Bac).

When she went to bed that night I sat up in front of the t.v., reclining in one motel chair with my feet up on another motel chair. I sipped rum-and-cola and tried to find something new in Johnny Carson.

And all of a sudden it began to sink in that the kid was no longer a boy, that she was now a girl, a precisely pubescent young lady.

If you expect me to announce at this juncture my sexual feelings for her you are 100% wrong. In fact, you have just admitted the perversion of your own erotic directions.

I did not gaze upon my daughter with lust. Rather, I walked into the Tucson foothills and delivered my rendition of the *Soliloquy* from *Carousel*.

A Profundity

On awaking, the kid said, "What a night of dreams and nightmares! Do you ever feel as if you were constantly moving back and forth among varying modes of reality?"

"Oh, no," I said, "my reality is always the only one that I have. It's just that reality is always moving in and out of its many and various modes."

Two Indian Chiefs

In Willcox, Arizona, the county seat of Cochise county, there is a Cochise hotel, a Cochise bar and grill, a Cochise general store, a Cochise boulevard, avenue, street and mews, and everything else is named for Cochise also.

I bet all the kids, even the white kids, are named Cochise.

These people must have loved the livin' be-jesus out of old Cochise.

It kind of makes you wonder what the fuck Geronimo must have done to piss them off.

On The Tom Mix Memorial Highway

We headed north, then, past the place where Tom Mix was killed in a car accident.

There was a modest monument to Tom Mix erected there, but I couldn't figure out why: what's so great about getting yourself killed in a car accident. I mean, trillions of people every day manage to get themselves killed in car accidents.

I think there should be monuments to the few who don't.

Awesome Canyon

As is always the case, the Salt River Canyon just awed the shit out of both of us. It also, as usual, scared me a little having to navigate that relatively narrow, windy, and steep highway with a young life in my care. I could remember having been even more scared, though, driving with hungover nerves the road into King's Canyon and not daring to drink a beer for fear of giving one or more of my wives or ex-wives ammunition to argue that I was an alcoholic and an unfit father.

At the top of the Salt River chasm, I stopped for gas and a beer and the kid wandered into an Apache Post. On my way back to the car I crossed paths with the ghost of the John Wayne of *The Searchers*. Even though both he and his horse were invisible, as ghosts tend to be more often than not, I could tell it was the John Wayne of *The Searchers* because he was whistling The Coasters' version of "I been searchin' ..." "Bear," John Wayne said, "where is the kid?"

"Oh, I gave her twenty bucks to go shopping in the Apache Trading Post. I don't imagine twenty bucks will go far even in a Trading Post nowadays though."

John grew agitated: "My God, man, don't you realize that poor little girl has no doubt already been

stolen away from you to be brought up as a squaw?!
And believe me, there are damn few Squaw
Chapters of the National Organization of Women.
We'd better start trailing her right now."

"How will we trail her?"

"We'll just follow the nearest pickup truck.
Don't you remember *Rancho Deluxe* where the old
Indian tells the young Indian that the curse of the
Indian is not the white man, but the pickup truck?
Damn smart Injun'!"

"Where do you figure they've taken her,
Duke?"

"Monument Valley."

"Monument Valley? Why Monument
Valley? Monument Valley isn't even Apache; it's
Navajos."

"How the hell do I know why? I just always
seem to end up in Monument Valley."

And with that The Duke went riding off into
the sunset ... which was not in the West, but to the
north, since that was the way to Monument Valley.
Duke looked very happy; he looked like a man with
a mission.

Oh, yeah, Duke was supposed to be invisible.
Well, in the course of our conversation, he had
gradually become visible. His horse was still
invisible however.

You give a little; I give a little.

Incidentally, John Wayne was no sooner out of sight than the kid emerged from the Indian Trading Post wearing numerous turquoise and silver necklaces, bracelets, and rings. She was also carrying a couple of woven blankets.

"Any problems?" I asked.

"Oh no," she gushed. "Everyone was just wonderful to me. I tried to talk them out of all the bargains they gave me, but they just wouldn't take no for an answer."

"No one tried to kidnap you?"

"Kidnap me? Have you been chewing some bad peyote?"

"No. Not I. Maybe someone else."

Although to tell you the truth, John Ford's movies, viewed today, seem less remarkable for the inevitable racial stereotyping than for an unusual, for its time, understanding of the historical plight of the Indian.

Trivia Question: What hit song was the flip-side for "Searchin' …"

"Young Blood"

For a slightly different view of the American Indians, I would recommend the films *Rainbow Bridge, Koyaanisquatsi,* and *The Seasons of a Navajo.*

For two views from the reservation, I would recommend the poems of Kirk Robertson and Nila Northson.

I would also recommend the fictions of Rudolfo Anaya and Rafael Zepeda.

I guess I wasn't quite done dropping names.

Easing the Epic Task

The next day in the car I said to the kid, "I know you don't drink, but do you ever take drugs?"

"No. Why would I?"

"Good," I said, "we can dispense with not only The Descent to Hades but the Lotus-eating Interlude as well."

A Not Very Subtle Chapter

We no sooner hit the High Plains than sure enough we got thumbed down for a ride by a Drifter.

"Where you headed, Old Buddy," I asked.

"Back," he said.

"You're looking kind of pale," I remarked.

"Pale," he said, "you should have seen my last horse. It was paler than its rider."

"What's that you're clutching in your fist?"

"A fistful of dollars."

"No wallet?"

"No pockets. I never learned to sew."

"No woman?"

"Too many of them. None of them could sew. All of them could shop."

"You sure you ain't starving to death?"

"I could use a little grub."

"What cuisine would suit your taste?"

"Italian."

I dropped him off at Ramon Rodriguez' Little Bit of Napoli and recommended the fry bread with garlic butter.

Trivia Question: On what novel by what author was the movie, *Hud*, based?

Trivia Answer: *Horseman, Pass By*, by Larry McMurtry.

Trivia Question: Where did McMurtry get that title?

Trivia Answer: From William Butler Yeats' epitaph for himself in "Under Ben Bulben:"

> cast a cold eye
> on life, on death
> Horseman, pass by.

Trivia Answer: Larry McMurtry
(What is the question?)

Trivia Question: Who also wrote *The Last Picture Show* and *Terms of Endearment*?

Trivia Answer: Brandon de Wilde
(What is the question?)

Trivia Question: Who played The Kid in
both *Shane* and *Hud*?

Trivia Question: Did William Butler Yeats write any westerns?

Trivia Answer: Yes, but they were all set in the West of Ireland.

Another Question: Why isn't Billy the Kid in this novel?

Another Answer: He is, by implication. He is what The Kid might have become if he had not had The Bear.

One Last Question: Why isn't *Blazing Saddles* spoofed in this spoof?

One Last Answer: Because *Blazing Saddles* is a spoof, and because this spoofer doesn't really enjoy spoofs, with the conspicuous exception of his own.

I do think *The Producers* is one of the funniest movies ever made.

And one of my daughters, who is much brighter than I am, thinks *Blazing Saddles* is one of the funniest movies ever made.

At this point I should add that I like my westerns straight, the same way I like my whiskey, but unfortunately I don't like my whiskey straight.

Invisible Means Of Support

"Bear," the kid said, "how have you supported yourself in the fifteen years since you so ingeniously solved *The Case of the Missing Blue Volkswagen?*"

"As a poet."

"As a poet? I don't think I've heard any of your poems."

"Here's one:

> Roses are red;
> Violets are blue.
> J. Alfred Prufrock
> was a wimp."

"Bear," the kid said, "I sure hope you're going to make enough on this case to be able to retire from the poetry racket."

This Novel Is Not A Satire; It Is A Series Of Tributes

"Bear," the kid asked, "why isn't Tom Horn in this novel?"

"I have too much respect for Tom Horn to put him in this novel. Tom Horn died for our sins. The other good guys in this mostly escaped with their skins, although Shane rode off clutching a shoulder wound of indeterminate severity that might in fact have been fatal."

"Bear," the kid asked, "what do you think of *High Noon*?"

"Great tune. Dubious lead, even though Hemingway's affection for him inclines me in his favor. The cowardice of the populace is such a powerful and obvious fact at any time in any place that it becomes, critically, a toss-up between its predictability and its unrelenting truth. Then there's Katy Jurado who always plays the woman that we would all like to fuck if it weren't that we all know that everyone else has already fucked her. And, finally, I'm not sure we really believe it. We are too aware of the criminality of criminals, of their viciousness, of the obvious fact that for whatever purpose they are a different breed than we are. Or that Gary Cooper was. And so we want to believe that Gary Cooper or any of us could, with a little bit of balls and a little bit of luck, have singlehandedly defeated that gang of prison-hardened criminals.

"But I don't think that ultimately—five minutes after we're out of the theatre—we really believe it. *Shane* is much more credible because *Shane* pits two professional gunfighters against one another, and the implication is that Shane is the best that ever lived, especially in the novel where Jack Shaefer has Shane instruct the Kid to "tell him (the father) that no man need be ashamed of being beaten by Shane." In the movie Shane is physically weaker than the father and has to resort to a sucker pistol-whipping to subdue the Kid's dad."

We Descended Then The 600 Foot Trail Into
Canyon de Chelly

And we waded the river to the Casa Blanca
pueblo ruins. We were surrounded by replacements
of the peach trees that Kit Carson had destroyed to
demoralize the Navajos and lead them out on the
first leg of what would become the near-genocidal
long walk across New Mexico.

I think Kit Carson was a pretty good guy, but
even good guys do bad things sometimes. The
overall sociopolitical climate has a lot to do with it.
Cf.: Nazi Germany. Cf.: The English support of
Margaret Thatcher as Bobbie Sands and others were
starving to death. I guess this episode could have
been headlined: *No More Gandhis*.

Cf.: The popular support of Ronald Reagan in
Grenada, Nicaragua, and Libya.

Not to mention his domestic policies.

Well, the surviving Navajo made it back to
Canyon de Chelly, at least, and the nearby town of
Chinle is thriving.

My daughter and I met the only hostile
Indians we were to encounter on the grass near the
Casa Blanca. But they were just kids really, junior
high school or less, just the typical gang mentality
that one is apt to encounter anywhere that kids are
left to hang around together without supervision and

87

form their own subculture. I had left all three guns in the car, but I did have my foldback knife in my pocket. I took it out, needlessly, to skin a peach, and the potential juvenile delinquents rode off. Gangs are always interested in *sure* things, not semi-sure things.

We waded back to the switchback trail flanked by a shepherdess with her flock of blankets and chops.

When we reached the cliff, the kid said, "I was beginning to wonder if you'd make it," but I told her, "I just set the speed record for my weight class."

At Last

Later that day we toured Monument Valley. The highlight was seeing Dennis Weaver and his horse flown by helicopter from the flat top of a monolith upon which they had been making commercials for an S. & L. whose image was entangled with the Great West.

That night we stayed in the trading post town of Kayenta, where I had once, assuming the age of ethnic paternalism to be long past, found myself bereft of alcohol with nearly a hundred miles in any direction to the next liquor store, if you could even count on it being open.

That time I ate a roast pork dinner at the Holiday Inn and threw it up.

This time we ate Mexican food at a café. The dinners were good, but neither cheap nor filling.

This time I had brought plenty of booze in the trunk of the Toyota. While I was falling asleep with a drink in front of the Johnny Carson Show, the kid said, "Look, I've enjoyed the scenery and the bullshit, but don't you think it's time we quit fucking around and went and saved my mother from the Bad Guys?"

I drained my drink and poured myself another. "Yes," I said, "we head north to Wyoming first thing in the morning."

The First Thing In The Morning

I was dreadfully hungover, so we didn't go anyplace.

But the following morning we did head north to Montana to save the kid's mom from the Bad Guys.

The Next Morning

After a hearty breakfast of egg-cheese-and-sausage McMuffins washed down with orange juice freshly reconstituted from fresh-frozen concentrate, we passed a gentleman with an eye patch thumbing by the side of the road. I barely reduced our speed as I drew and plugged him.

"So much for the Cyclops episode," I said, and I shot all the farm animals for the next few miles as well, the better to dispose of Circe.

Calypso was already the joint property of the Cousteau Society and John Denver.

The Death of Hondo

We stopped for gas in the town of Mexican League Baseball Cap, Utah. There was a mini-mart at the station and in front of the mini-mart was a phony hitching post. With one foot up on the hitching post stood a cowboy who was phony in every way except for his six-shooter.

A much scruffier cowboy was kind of shufflin' along towards the hitchin' post, and his scruffier-yet dawg was scampering and barking along a good twenty yards ahead of him.

The mutt came scurrying up to the hitching post and began nipping at the ankles of the 90% phony cowboy who had been 50% resting on it. The 90% phony cowboy brought down his leg that had been resting on the hitching post, and with it he sent the scrofulous mutt skidding about a hundred yards down the highway and off into the sagebrush.

At that, the kid drew one of my guns from one of my holsters, ran towards the mini-mart, and shouting, "You shouldn't ought to ha' done that," shot the 90% phony cowboy in the left ventricle. Since he had been suffering, undiagnosed, from a defective right ventricle, there was little for him to say except, "That's about it for me, I guess."

It took Hondo about twenty minutes to traverse the final ten yards to the hitching post.

When he had, he drew and fired three quick bullets into the 90% phony cowboy.

"You asshole," the kid said, "he was already dead as the last Chernobyl bond issue."

Hondo turned to her and said, "Yeah, he's dead all right. He's dead because you stole my punchline and you upstaged my action. Now you die, sweetknickers."

She reached for her gun and I reached for mine, but Hondo had caught us off guard and there was no way I could have saved her. A volley exploded just as Hondo was pulling the trigger, and his bullets fell back from that heaven that he was also most likely undestined to reach.

Between the gas pumps stood the kid, the kid's brother, whose name of course had to be Joey, just as his twin sister's was, appropriately, Josie.

The Three Of Us

There wouldn't be much stopping us now, but there were still minor obstacles standing in our path before the rescuing of the kids' mother.

In one mountain range we encountered Clark Gable trying to lasso wild stallions, over the protestations of Mongtomery Clift and Marilyn Monroe. We did him the favor of lassoing Monty and Marilyn, but only after he promised to release Viva Zapata's white horse who had strayed a bit north of the border and who will return once again to lead the poor when their burden becomes unbearable.

In a geographically inappropriate section of Colorado, we arrived just after an enormous bully had beaten Marlon Brando in arm wrestling with giant scorpions under their fists. He wanted to play the same game with us and we shrugged why not. He was so exhausted from the Herculean struggle that he succumbed with ease to first me and then Joey and then Josie. We left him to sweat out three times the scorpion venom that Marlon had absorbed.

Finally, high upon the flatness of a mesa we came face to face with the one bad guy who got away in *One-Eyed Jacks*. His horse looked exhausted; he appeared even more so. "It's not easy being always on the run, not pleasant knowing all the western fans in America are out to get you, their sense of hubris and nemesis still unsatisfied. Go ahead—I've been expecting you and I've lived this scene in my mind a million times—put me out of my misery!"

Whom the fuck did he think he was conning? Did he really think we'd never read *Tom Sawyer* or the *Uncle Remus Stories*? We said, "Okay, we'll be glad to oblige you," and just as he opened his mouth to protest that he'd only been jiving us, we blasted him and the horse he rode in on right over the cliff.

Homages

We stopped to pay homage to the little Ezra Pound collection in the Hailey, Idaho, public library.

We stopped to pay homage to the Hemingway Memorial outside of Sun Valley, Idaho, facing north towards the last great American wilderness: "Best of all he loved the fall..." began his eulogy for a fellow hunter early deceased.

We drove by the house of his eldest son, Jack Bumby Schatz Hemingway in Ketchum, Idaho. Jack is the father of the famous Hemingway granddaughters and the most appreciative of his father of the Hemingway sons. That Hemingway loved Jack's mother and despised theirs may have something to do with this.

We had a drink in a now-deserted ski bar with a friendly barmaid from California.

Then we made tracks for the Grand Tetons.

A Question Of Locale

The events upon which *Shane* (and *Heaven's Gate* and numerous other historical or semi-historical accounts) were based occurred in what were known as the Johnson County Wars. I don't even know where Johnson County is, but I know the background landscape of the film *Shane* is the Grand Tetons pated up behind what one may presume to have been the Jackson Hole of a hundred years ago. I may be very wrong about the history and geography—and I would direct you to my former colleagues Roscoe Buckland and Audrey Peterson for a more accurate account, but the place to which we traveled was the valley of the Tetons, of the Snake and Gros Ventre rivers, of Jenny Lake and Lizard Creek and those high horned horny nightmare-Oedipal Tits.

Then The Kids Said, "Tell Us About Your Own Father."

He would never have won any Father-of-the-Year awards, but I know he loved me and I know that I loved him. He made many sacrifices for me.

I am conscious that in my later years I have tried to be to my children some small reflection of the father that my father was to me.

I hope and trust that my own sons, should they choose to have children, will be a better father to their children than I have managed to be to them.

This Book Is Dedicated To My Father

who died one week before my graduation from high
school.

I Waited Until The Children Were Asleep

And then I went to the Toyota, extracted a screwdriver, and withdrew a suitcase from within the secret compartment in the wagon section.

I took from the suitcase one six-shooter in one holster on one belt. I took from the suitcase my proper attire, deerskin, fringed, booted, and spurred, and with my head properly covered.

In the dark I removed my clown costume: the three gun belts, the one chap, the 11-gallon hat, etc. They had served their purpose. Now I burned them in an arroyo.

I donned the appropriate garb of the real gunfighter. I strapped the single belt around my waist. It felt as though I had never been unclothed of them.

I had inserted my key in the ignition of the Toyota wagon, when a horse of brown skin and white mane came galloping towards me out of the darkness.

I mounted the stallion and we cantered at an even pace towards the town.

I felt I was being followed, but I did not look back.

The craggy-titted peaks loomed to my right. I did not know if they were with me, but I knew they were not against me.

I Knew I Was Being Watched Over

I was being watched over by Edit Piaf.

I was being watched over by Marlene Dietrich.

I was being watched over by George Stevens.

I was being watched over by Ernest Hemingway.

I really didn't need a whole helluva lot of other people watching over me.

had composed the score for my ride into town.

Ben Johnson rode out to meet me halfway and warn me that the cards were stacked against me.

Elisha Cook, Jr. was dead. He was very dead, in fact, having been killed in *The Big Sleep* also.

Brandon de Wilde was dead in real life, God rest his very young soul.

I don't know whether Van Heflin had run off with a younger woman or whether he had never woken up from the knock upside the head that Alan Ladd had given him with his pistol.

Edgar Buchanan was still around but he was looking rather pale and considering an offer from the Beverly Hillbillies.

Jack Palance—Jack Wilson was still alive and waiting for me. I felt a shiver up my spine and thought of pulling up on the horse and having a swig from the bottle that I trusted was secreted within my sidebag. No, I decided, I really don't need it.

As I Draw Near The Close

of this novella, I hear on the jazz station, KLON, from the venerable jazz disc jockey, Chuck Niles, that Benny Goodman, the man who brought jazz to Carnegie Hall, has died of a cardiac arrest.

This weekend's Playboy Jazz Festival at the Hollywood Bowl will be dedicated to him.

I took my kids to the first Playboy Jazz Festival at the Hollywood Bowl and Benny Goodman, a whitey-with-experience-who-knew-how-to-rise-to-the-occasion stole the show.

Talent will always transcend prejudices.

If this novella were not already dedicated to my father, I would be tempted to dedicate it to Benny Goodman.

Oh, I Also Meant To Mention That All The Gunfights And Other Acts Of Violence Up To This Point In The Novella Were Faked

Dum-dum bullets were used. No one actually died. No one was seriously injured. In other words, I, The Bear, have never before in my life held in my hand a gun with real bullets in it. I have never before killed or injured anyone or even struck anyone in violence.

You can see how this riding-into-town bullshit is kind of a big deal for me.

Okay, Let's Cut The Crap

I hitched my faithful horse to the post and pushed my way through the dutch doors into Crapton's Saloon.

The Patriarch said, "We have no quarrel with you Sh--, I mean, Bear; we can make you a very generous offer to join our side, and our side is the side of laissez-faire economics, of the open range, of frontier justice, of The Real Man."

"I *am* The Real Man," I said, "and I am *not* on your side. I am on the side of the underdog, the bottom-dog, the true aristocracy of talent and energy and genius and vision and sacrifice and caring and responsibility for ourselves and our loved ones. You should recognize these qualities, Patriarch, because you once possessed them, way back decades ago before you realized you held the power and could manipulate and engineer the deals and buy the police and politicians and institutionalize the rhetoric and, in general, make a mockery of laissez-faire and transform it into Tammany Hall dictatorship."

"Bear," the Patriarch said, "You are the last person I would have suspected of seeking to accomplish The Twilight of the Elephant. You are a traitor to your manhood."

"Patriarch," I said, "you are only seconds from paying for that last remark. Let me now state, as I have so often, that I have four daughters and three sons and I want the best and fairest world possible for all of them."

"Then you are my enemy also," I heard, and turned to face the Matriarch.

"My name," she said, "is Sarah St. Lawrence."

"Where is the Kids' mother?" I said.

"She is a prisoner of both the Patriarch and the Matriarch. And you will have to kill both to release her."

"Then that," I said, "is what I'm prepared to do."

"Easier said than done," said Sarah St. Lawrence. "First you have to draw against The Terrible Twosome, Jack Wilson and Jackie Wilsonia."

They were sitting behind a card table grinning like a pair of Great White Sharks.

"Surprise," they laughed, "you never knew you had two döppelgangers, did you?"

"No," I admitted, "I thought one was more than enough."

"You don't have to draw, Bear," they said. "We'd love to have you join up with us."

"I think I read that line somewhere. Like when Satan had the hubris to solicit Christ in the desert."

"Then draw, Bear."

"I never draw except in self-defense," I said, or in defense of others. I can even swallow insults and walk away from provocations. But one thing I'd really like to ask you two—oh servants of the Patriarch and Matriarch—is which of you is the biggest Cunt?"

They went for their guns simultaneously, and I planted a bullet in the chest of each of them. Their chairs went over backwards rather pathetically.

I allowed myself one great sigh of relief when all of a sudden I heard, "Watch out, Bear," and I dropped to my knees and sent The Patriarch and The Matriarch and two of their henchmen/henchwomen tumbling out of the attic.

I thought my ass was grass, then, because I was out of bullets and there were chickenshit yellowbellied assassins trying to find their niche in every nook and cranny of the goddamn bar and general store, but a fireflood of automatic weapon fire broke out behind me, obliterating the bad guys and turning the doused structure into a raging bull of a raging inferno.

"You left your key in the ignition of the Toyota," the kids said. "We couldn't sleep and we got up to ask you to read us a bedtime story, but when you weren't there we decided we'd better ride into town and waste the rest of the bad guys.

Somehow we managed to divide your three guns, already altered into semi-automatic weapons, into one-and-a-half automatic weapons each, but don't ask us how we did it. Now, will you come home and read us a bedtime story?"

"No," I said, "I'm afraid I can't. I'm afraid I have to be getting back to my own wives and kids."

"You mean you have to ride back to L.A. and shoot the shit out of the bad guys."

"Oh no," I said, "I'm afraid it's not as simple as that. No, it involves mortgages and brownie meetings and infidelities and oft-overlooked fidelities and burglar alarms and smoke alarms and insurance policies and P.T.A. meetings and income taxes and Disneyland and cable T.V. and bosses and subordinates and parking tickets and seat belts and exercycles and pants you have to belt beneath your beer-belly and consequently you are always tripping over the cuffs."

"What's the worst of it all, Bear?"

"The worst indignity of all is the seat belts."

"Bear, they got you in the shoulder!"

"Yeah, but one third of them were aiming at my balls, and one third at my heart. I'll settle for one hit in the shoulder."

"Bear, you know when you say things like that you're opening yourself up to charges of paranoia and opening this narrative up to flights of critical psychoanalytic excess."

"Shit, I hope critics will take this narrative into whatever flight their pterodactyl-like and often brainwashed capacities will allow them. I would especially ask that no one utter a word of praise or condemnation of this narrative without acquiring a familiarity with the works of Norman Holland, I.A. Richards, Freud, Jung, Joseph Campbell, Robert Graves, Michael Foucault, Lévi-Strauss, Jacques Lacan, Roland Barthes, Jacques Derrida, Charles May, and the numerous writers cited within the text. All I ask is that your criticisms of my work be no less informed than my criticisms of yours."

"But how can all these theoreticians be right?"

"They can't all be 100% right, but none of them is 100% wrong either."

"On a more personal level, Bear, won't you miss us?"

"I will awake in the middle of the night sweating and shaking and racked with remorse. I will want to come to your aid but I will know that only you can come to your aid and only I can come to mine. But, yeah, if you ever need me, call collect, and I'll do likewise."

"Your horse looks tired … can we get you a fresh one?"

"No, I think I'll just drive back in the old Toyota wagon."

"Bear, were Jack Wilson and Jackie Wilsonia fast?"

"Yes, they were fast. They were very fast. But they were also full of shit."

Nearing The Finale

"Wouldn't you like to meet Mom?"

"I have the feeling that I already have. But give her my best, will you? And tell her I'm sorry it just wasn't possible to stick around."

Getting <u>Very</u> Close To The Finale

"Shane, whatever happened to our father, Joe?"

"<u>I</u> am your father Joe."

"We thought you were Shane."

"I <u>am</u> Shane."

The Finale

"Bear, will we ever meet again?"

"Oh, I don't know, I suppose it could happen; I suppose that anything could happen; but it doesn't really matter because we are already a part of each other and a part of many other people and that is all that we can do to lend ourselves a modicum of immortality, but the more you think about it, it ain't exactly the proverbial chopped liver."

"Bear, we love you."

"I love you too."

Final Finale

As I am setting down my pen, I hear the knob of the bedroom door turning. It is my little boy, who says, "I can't sleep."

"Okay, big guy," I say, "you can sit up with me for a while."

I take my drink and my little boy to the couch and we watch some MTV, which he prefers even to the Disney Channel. When I get up to pour myself another drink, he plays the Whoopie Cushion Trick on me. This involves my pretending not to notice the cushions he has piled where I have been sitting and my then emitting a loud Bronx Cheer when I lower myself onto them. After he stops laughing, I say, "How was school today," and he says, "Darby was mean to me again. He pulled my hair and he tried to stick his fingers in my eyes."

I have seen Darby in action at a birthday party. The kid is a good argument for early genetic testing and preventative detention of the violently disposed. "Darby hurt you *again*?" I say.

"Every day."

"Why don't you just not play with him?"

"I like to play with him most of the time. He's my friend. But then all of a sudden he gets angry and hurts me. I wish he wouldn't."

114

"You know, it's all right with me if you hurt him back. I'll even teach you how to hurt him so he'll remember it for a while."

But I know what his answer will be: "My teachers tell me not to hurt him back. Mommy tells me not to hurt him back."

So I hold him and tell him how much I love him and what a good boy he is and how proud of him I am, and after I get him back in bed I leave his mother one note about the house we are trying to buy and another about how the people who are teaching my son to be a pacifist do not seem to be doing anything to protect him and how I am about ready to start telling him what I *know* to be best for him, not what Women's Studies has made its most recent theoretical fad. I remind her that it is the women who are studying self-defense and carrying mace nowadays and that in our seventeen years together she has never seen me strike another person, but she has never seen another person strike me either, and that this is not because I have been studious to avoid those places where tensions run high.

I finish my drink, leave the notes on the breakfast counter, and collapse drunkenly into bed.

When I awake in the morning my wife and kids will be gone to Knott's Berry Farm. (I asked my wife if she would rather have me come with them or give her the money it would cost me, and she took the money.)

I will be very hungover—headache and dry heaves, the works. I will be sorry I left the drunken, polarizing note rather than waiting to broach the topic in a soberer, more diplomatic, and generally more effective manner.

I will have to get through the nervous time until the cocktail hour—try to do at least a little work and maybe keep down a little food, a few vitamins.

Later it will be all right to drink, but not to overdo it. If I go out to a bar, I will not wear a gun. I don't even own one. I've never fired a live round in my life.

I do, however, on occasion carry in my pocket a lock-back knife, one just short enough not to qualify as a concealed weapon.

I've never used that either, though.

I will hope that I feel good enough tomorrow to go for a good long swim which will remind me that it was not so long ago that I was lean, athletic, and heavily muscled—the kid who in senior year of high school was co-captain of the football, basketball and track teams, the guy who played basketball and lifted weights well into his thirties.

Maybe I will call an old girlfriend or a potentially young one.

Maybe I will just stay home with my kids.
I will go on with my life.

About the Author

Gerald Locklin has published over one hundred volumes of poetry, fiction, and literary essays including *Charles Bukowski: A Sure Bet*, (Water Row Press) and *Go West, Young Toad*, (Water Row Press). Charles Bukowski called him "One of the great undiscovered talents of our time." *The Oxford Companion to Twentieth Century Literature in the English Language* calls him "a central figure in the vitality of Los Angeles writing." His works have been widely translated and he has given countless readings here and in England. He is a Professor Emeritus at California State University, Long Beach.